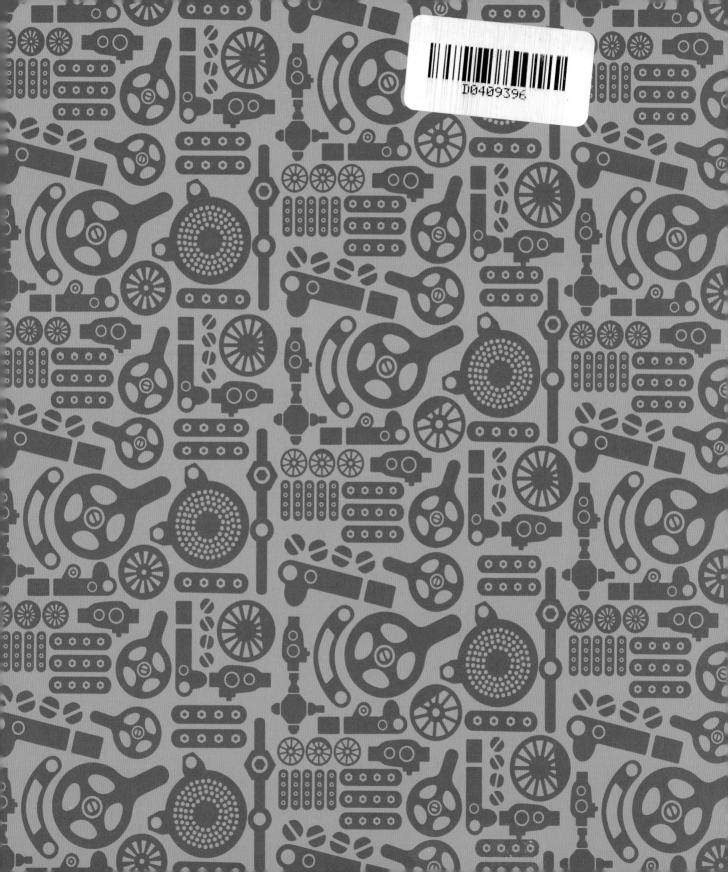

EGMONT

We bring stories to life

This edition published in Great Britain 2012 by Dean,
an imprint of Egmont UK Limited
239 Kensington High Street, London W8 6SA

Thomas the Tank Engine & Friends™

CREATED BY BRITT ALLCROFT

HiT entertainment

ISBN 978 0 6035 6671 4
51282/1
Printed in China

Thomas and the Green Controller

Based on *The Railway Series* by The Rev. W. Awdry

It was a quiet day at Tidmouth Sheds. Percy was all alone.

Suddenly, The Fat Controller's car pulled up. Percy was very surprised when Lady Hatt and her friends got out of the car instead!

"Sir Topham is sick," she announced, grandly. "He has lost his voice."

Percy was worried. "I hope he finds it soon," he peeped.

Lady Hatt read out a list of jobs from The Fat Controller. "Gordon is to collect coaches of china from Knapford and take them to the Docks . . . he must go very slowly."

"Slow cars," peeped Percy.

"James is to shunt trucks in the Coal Yards . . . he must be as busy as a bee," Lady Hatt went on. "And Toby is to take visitors to the Scottish Castle . . . he must go as fast as Gordon's Express!"

"Gordon's Express," puffed Percy.

"You're in charge now, Percy," said Lady Hatt.

Off Percy chuffed.

He found Gordon first. "The Fat Controller has lost his voice," puffed Percy. "So I am Controller until he finds it!"

Gordon was surprised.

Percy tried hard to remember what Lady Hatt had said. "You must pull very slow cars!" he peeped.

"Oh, the indignity!" huffed Gordon.

Percy had a lot to do and a lot to remember!

Next, Percy found James at the Washdown. "James, you must be a busy bee!" he peeped.

James gasped. "Do you mean I have to be yellow and black?" he whistled angrily. James wanted to keep his red paint!

"Yes, James," said Percy. "I am Controller! Engines must do as they are told." Then he puffed away.

Next, Percy found Toby. "Toby, you must pull Gordon's Express!" he told him. "That's your job."

Toby was very puzzled.

Later, Percy decided it was time to check on his engines.

He knew that's what The Fat Controller would do.

Some children were waiting on the bridge.
Percy peeped, "hello".

But the children were looking at the track where
Gordon was puffing slowly down the line.

The children began to laugh. "Look at Gordon,"
they cried, "what a slowcoach!"

Then James stopped at the signal.

His splendid red paintwork had been painted with yellow and black stripes.

"Who is that giant stripy bee?" the children laughed.

Finally, Toby huffed in with the heavy Express.

It was very hard work for a little engine like him, and Toby was tired.

"My axles ache!" poor Toby wheeshed to James.

Gordon, James and Toby heard the children laughing. And they saw Percy watching.

Gordon called out to Percy, "I am supposed to be the fastest engine on Sodor! Not the slowest!" he huffed.

"I'm supposed to be the reddest engine," moaned James. "Now no one knows who I am!"

"I'm only a steam tram," Toby puffed. "The Express is too heavy for me to pull."

Percy was worried. He knew he had made lots of mistakes.

Then Thomas puffed up. "What's wrong, Percy?" he asked his friend.

"Please help me, Thomas," sighed Percy. "I can't remember what Lady Hatt told me. All the engines are doing the wrong jobs."

Thomas thought for a moment. "You must go back over your tracks," he puffed. "You might see things that will help you remember."

Percy thought that was a very good idea.

Thomas and Percy pulled into Knapford Station.

"Gordon and slow cars," puffed Percy.

Suddenly, Percy saw crates of china waiting on the platform.

"That's it!" Percy cried. "Gordon is to take the china to the Docks. He must pull his coaches very slowly!"

Percy and Thomas puffed into the Coal Yards.

"James must be a busy bee," Percy said, slowly.

There were lots of grumbling coal trucks waiting to be shunted.

"That's it – James is to shunt lots of trucks! So, he must be as busy as a bee!" smiled Percy.

Finally, Percy and Thomas arrived at the station.

"Toby must pull Gordon's Express," puzzled Percy.

Suddenly, Percy saw a group of visitors, waiting on the platform.

"That's it!" Percy cried. "Toby is to take visitors to the Scottish Castle! He has to go as fast as Gordon's Express!"

Later, The Fat Controller came to the Sheds.

"You have done well, little Percy," he smiled.
"I'm very pleased."

"And I'm very pleased that you've found your voice."
Percy peeped, happily. "I just hope you never lose
it again!"